D0509906

My First Disney Story

This is a book for you to share with your child time and time again.

Read the story aloud, pointing to the words as you go. Encourage your child to look at the pictures, and talk about the story and what she* can see. Ask questions about the action, and point out favourite characters. If your child is familiar with the story, she will enjoy telling you what is going to happen next! Encourage her to tell the story in her own words.

Above all, have fun sharing this favourite Disney tale with your child.

* To avoid the clumsy he/she and his/her we have referred to the child as she. All the books are, of course, equally suited to boys and girls, and all children will have their favourites.

A catalogue record for this book is available from the British Library

Published by Ladybird Books Ltd
A subsidiary of the Penguin Group
A Pearson Company
LADYBIRD and the device of a Ladybird are trademarks of Ladybird Books Ltd Loughborough Leicestershire UK

Based on the book by Dodie Smith. Published by Heinemann Limited

Roger's new wife Anita had a pet Dalmatian too. Her name was Perdita.

Soon after the wedding Pongo and Perdita's first puppies were born – fifteen of them. Roger, Anita and Nanny the housekeeper were delighted.

Anita's friend Cruella De Vil was pleased as well. She wanted to buy all of them! But Roger wouldn't let her.

Cruella was determined to have the puppies. She sent two bad men, Horace and Jasper Badun, to dognap them.

They waited for Roger and Anita to take Pongo and Perdita for a walk. Then they forced their way into the house. Nanny tried to stop them, but they managed to take the puppies away.

The police searched up and down the country. But the puppies were nowhere to be found. At last Pongo decided to try the Twilight Bark.

His deep bark was answered by a Great Dane. Soon the news about the puppies began to spread all over the country.

When word reached a sheepdog called Colonel, he was very worried. So were his friends, a horse called Captain and a cat called Tibs.

“I heard puppies barking at the old De Vil house,” said Tibs.

Colonel and Tibs crept up to the house and saw the puppies with Horace and Jasper Badun.

The news was barked to London, and the Dalmatians set off straightaway.

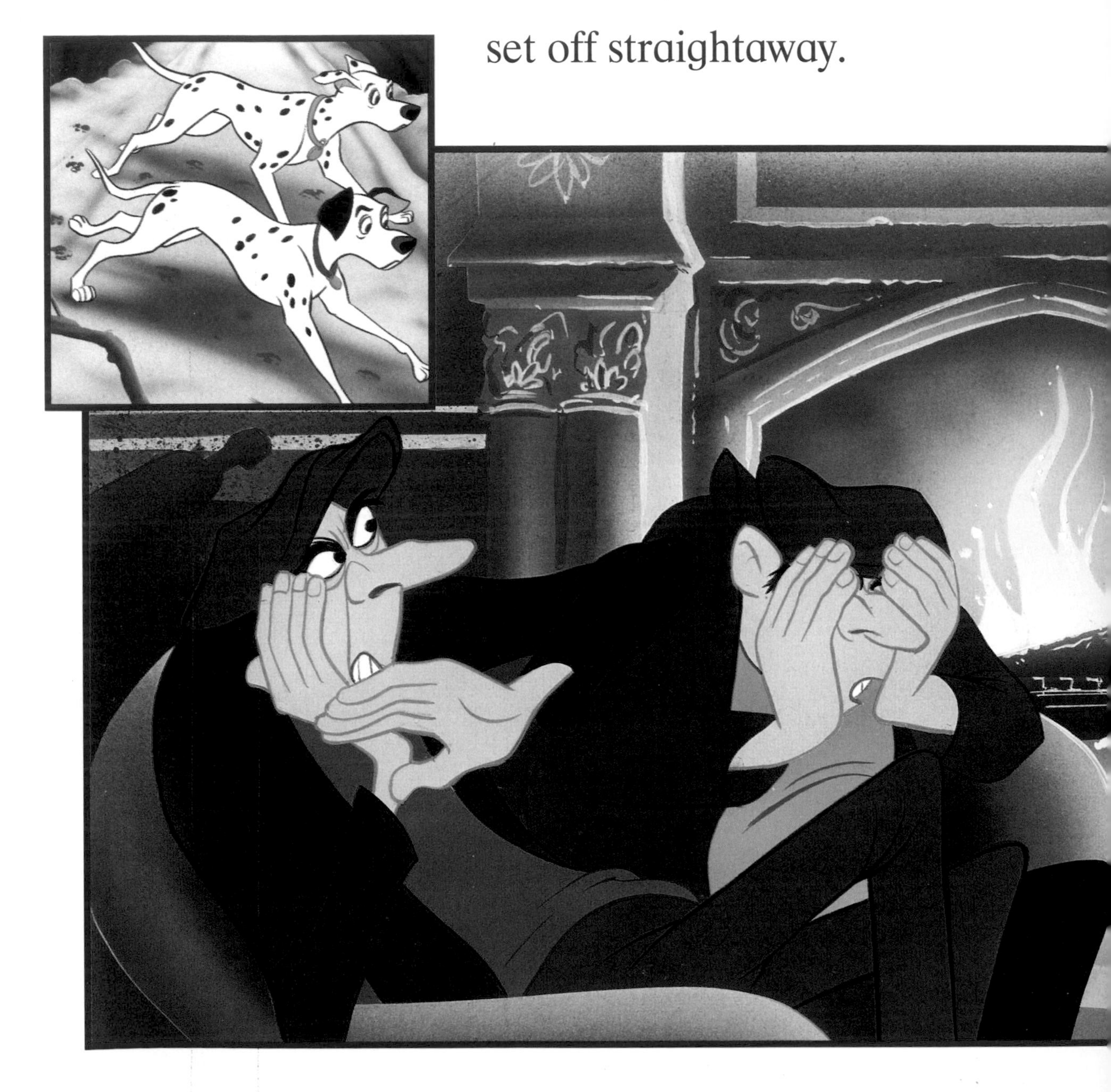

Meanwhile Tibs was watching the house. When Cruella De Vil turned up, he crept closer to listen. He heard her say, “I want their spotty skins for fur coats!” And with that, she left.

Tibs was horrified. How could anyone be so cruel? He must rescue those puppies.

He crept into the house and whispered to the nearest puppy, "You must all escape – Cruella is after your coats!" The puppies followed him upstairs to hide.

Perdita and Pongo arrived just as Horace and Jasper found the puppies again. Perdita attacked Horace, and Pongo tore at Jasper's trousers.

While the fight was going on, Tibs led the puppies out of the house.

Perdita and Pongo left Horace and Jasper and hurried after the puppies.

“Are all our puppies here?” asked Perdita. They counted. There were ninety nine puppies!

“We can’t leave the other puppies behind,” said Perdita. “Come on, we’ll take them all back to London.” The Dalmatians set off, leaving pawprints in the snow.

Cruella and Horace and Jasper were soon on their trail. To throw Cruella off the scent, the puppies rolled in some soot that made them look like black Labradors.

Unluckily, the soot came off when it snowed, and Cruella was after them again. But when Horace and Jasper's van crashed into her car, the chase was over. At last the puppies were safe!

Back home at last, Roger, Anita and Nanny hugged the tired puppies. Roger started to count.

"There are one hundred and one Dalmatians here, counting Pongo and Perdita. We'll have to buy a big house in the country."

So that's what they did!